LOST POTATOES

A Harrowing Tale of Two Potatoes on the Lam

Written and Illustrated by

Laurie Jean Harlan

AuthorHouse™
1663 Liberty Drive
Bloomington, IN 47403
www.authorhouse.com
Phone: 1 (800) 839-8640

Published by AuthorHouse 02/29/2016

ISBN: 978-1-5049-8025-8 (sc)
ISBN: 978-1-5049-8027-2 (hc)
ISBN: 978-1-5049-8026-5 (e)

Library of Congress Control Number: 2016902591

Print information available on the last page.

authorHOUSE®

Lost Potatoes
is dedicated to my sisters,
Diana Lynne and Elaine Kay. May you
never again lose anything you love.

A special thanks to everyone who helped me
make Lost Potatoes happen. Jay and Jing
Harlan, Lori J Dietz, The Gudgel Family, Kevin
Harlan, Sarah Symons, Mary Jane Harbath,
Jude and Mike Dennis, Lynnette James, Laura
Lee Ellen Johnson, Ally Steele, Ken Zufelt, Tony
and Kristen Erickson, Kathi Seid, The Kruck
Family, Rick and Paula Vogel and everyone else
who believed in me and my little dream.

When Chip went to Mr. Spud's grocery store, he bought two potatoes and not a thing more.

Chip LOVED potatoes. He liked nothing better. With
a dollop of cream and a smidgeon of cheddar.

What he didn't know as a matter of fact, there
was a great big hole in his potato sack.
As he made his way home those two potatoes found
their way through the big hole and down to the ground.

He was halfway home when he decided to sneak
a look at his taters, just one tiny peek.
But when he opened the bag and
saw them both GONE!!!......

He threw a HUGE tantrum on Ms. Russet's lawn!
"Where can they be? Where can they BE?"

"Hmmm...just a minute now. Let me see.
I'll turn back around, go back into town.
I'll find those two 'tatoes. I'll look all around".
Just then the garden club walked by.
"I'll ask those nice ladies, it's sure worth a try".

"So sorry to interrupt you ladies, but I seem
to have lost my lovely potaytees".
"Lost your potatoes?", cried Mrs. Au Gratin. "My
goodness my dear, you must feel quite rotten".

And indeed he did as he turned back around,
running fast as he could Chip headed to town.

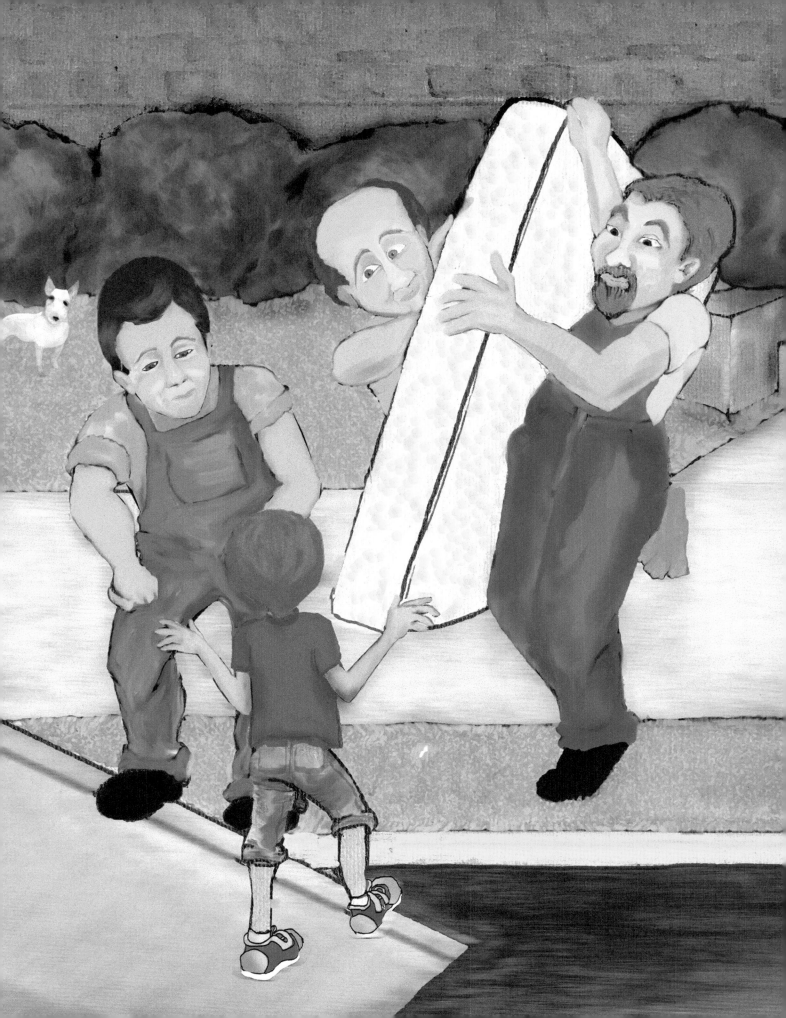

Mr. Scalloped was working with
some *big, brawny* movers.
Chip asked them per chance had
they *seen* his two tubers.
"We've been moving stuff all day, but move your
potatoes? Not a chance kid, NO WAY"!

He asked little JoJo who was really quite naughty.
She just blew him a raspberry and
said she had to go potty.

"Where can they BE?", Chip loudly cried. "I've looked so hard, I've tried and I've tried"!
"You'll NEVER find them!", yelled mean Mr. Fries. As he glared and he stared with his grumpy old eyes.

At last by the daycare called Miss Tater's Tots,
Chip plopped himself down and suddenly spots,
under a bush all dark and all dim, his two
potatoes' eyes looking right back at him.

"I found them!" Chip yelled to the gathering crowd. He gave them sloppy kisses which were embarrassingly loud.

"This bag is just perfect", said the grocer Mr. Spud.
"So sorry the last one was such a *big dud*".
"And maybe lose them again?! Not a
chance! OH pSHAW!!!...".

So in the middle of Main Street.
Chip ate both of them...
RAW!

Laurie Jean Harlan grew up in Michigan and now
resides in Vancouver, Washington. Self-taught with
a love for art, she wrote "Lost Potatoes" as a
fledgling leap into the publishing world. Her years as
a nanny spinning yarns and telling tales have been
the main inspiration in bringing this story to life.

CPSIA information can be obtained
at www.ICGtesting.com
Printed in the USA
LVOW05s2024230316
480491LV00017B/83/P

9 781504 980258